Guinea Pig Superstar

Lucy Daniels

With special thanks to Tabitha Jones. For Bel.

Illustrations by Jo Anne Davies for Artful Doodlers

ORCHARD BOOKS

First published in Great Britain in 2019 by The Watts Publishing Group

1 3 5 7 9 10 8 6 4 2

Text copyright © Working Partners, 2019
Illustrations copyright © Working Partners, 2019

The moral rights of the author and illustrator have been asserted.

A CIP catalogue record for this book
is available from the British Library.

ISBN 978 1 40835 410 0

Printed and bound in Great Britain by CPI Group (UK) Ltd, Croydon, CR0 4YY

The paper and board used in this book are made from wood from responsible sources.

MIX
Paper from
responsible sources
FSC® C104740
www.fsc.org

Orchard Books
An imprint of
Hachette Children's Group
Part of The Watts Publishing Group Limited
Carmelite House
50 Victoria Embankment
London EC4Y 0DZ

An Hachette UK Company
www.hachette.co.uk
www.hachettechildrens.co.uk

CONTENTS

CHAPTER ONE

"I've found another one!" called Amelia. She lifted a smooth brown egg from a clump of grass and held it up to show Sam and Dervla.

"I've got one too!" Amelia's best friend Sam cried, his arm down the side of the chicken coop. "It's tricky to reach!"

He let out a grunt, stretching further. "Got it!" he called, easing himself up.

"Pop them in here with the rest," Dervla said, holding out her basket. It was already more than half full.

Sam and Amelia had volunteered to help Dervla — a friend of Amelia's grandmother — collect the morning's eggs. Amelia hadn't expected it to be quite so much like an Easter egg hunt! A few of Dervla's hens had laid eggs in the nest boxes inside their wooden coop, but most seemed to prefer just about anywhere else. They'd even found an egg in a wheelbarrow!

As Amelia headed towards Dervla, plump chickens bobbed out of her way, clucking and cooing to each other as they went. Amelia noticed one little chicken, speckled and fluffy, standing by her foot. It gazed up at her with its head cocked and a hopeful look in its eye.

"Sorry," Amelia said. "I haven't got any food for you." The hen stepped closer, nudging her leg with its head.

"Ava likes people," Dervla said. "Try stroking her."

Amelia crouched and ran her hand over Ava's soft feathers. The hen let out a rumble of contented little clucks.

"Cool," Sam said. He bent to stroke a plump brown chicken, but it pecked at his fingers. "Ouch! I guess that one isn't so friendly!" he said, rubbing his hand.

Outside the hen enclosure, Sam's shaggy white Westie pup, Mac, snuffled at the wire fence, his ears flat to his head and his stumpy tail wagging.

SQUAWK! The fat hen that had pecked Sam flapped towards the little dog, clucking angrily. She pecked at Mac's nose through the fence, making him leap back with a yelp.

Dervla let out a chuckle, her blue eyes glinting. "He's wise to keep his distance," she said. "The hens all have their own personalities.

Some are friendly, like Ava, but old Magda here's a bit of a battle-axe. Now, how many eggs did your mum want, Sam?"

"Twelve, please," he answered, digging in his pocket for the money. His parents owned a local bed and breakfast and bought Dervla's eggs for their customers' breakfasts.

As Dervla placed a dozen eggs in a cardboard box, Amelia watched the hens, trying to imagine what they might be saying to each other. They mostly kept together, pecking at the ground. But a few hens, mainly small speckled ones that Amelia hadn't noticed before, kept their distance from the rest of the flock.

"Do you have some new chickens, Dervla?" Amelia asked.

Dervla grinned. "Well spotted! A dozen arrived the day before yesterday from a local egg factory that is shutting down. It's a good thing too." Her eyes turned unusually stern. "They were treated horribly there, cooped up in tiny spaces with no real sunlight. They're much better off here." She sighed. "I only wish I could have adopted more. There are plenty left at the rehoming centre, but I've got my hands full with this lot."

As if to prove her right, a racket of screeching and flapping erupted at her feet. "Oh dear!" Dervla said. "Magda's started another fight."

Amelia and Sam rushed at the hens, waving their arms. Most scattered, but Magda held her ground, jabbing her beak at a scrappy speckled bird. The smaller hen tried pecking back, but Magda flapped upwards, clucking and swiping with sharp claws.

"Hey! Stop that!" Sam cried, putting his arm between the two birds. The smaller chicken turned tail to scramble away, but Magda chased after it. *Oh!* Amelia noticed something which made

her heart squeeze. The fleshy red comb
on the smaller bird's head was torn and
bleeding.

Amelia pushed Magda firmly away
and scooped the speckled bird into her
arms. The injured hen barely seemed to
weigh anything at all, and its body was
strangely stiff beneath its feathers.

"Look, she's hurt!" Amelia said, showing the torn, red frill on the bird's head to Sam and Dervla.

"Poor thing!" Sam said.

Dervla shook her head sadly. "It's never easy for new hens joining a flock," she said. "Chickens like to have a pecking order – it's a kind of ranking system that decides who gets the best food, and who's the boss. Magda's in charge and she's decided that these new hens aren't welcome here at all. Poor Lola here seems to be taking the brunt of her fury." Dervla gently touched the speckled bird's torn comb. Lola let out a low, grumbling sound. "Ooh! That does

look sore," Dervla said.
"I think we'd better
take her to Animal
Ark."

Even though she
was worried about
Lola, Amelia shared
an excited look
with Sam. They had
both recently become official helpers
at Animal Ark, the local veterinary
surgery.

"We'll come with you!" Amelia said.

"We can look after Lola on the way!"
Sam chimed in.

Dervla smiled. "That would be a great

help." She turned to her hens with a comical frown and shook her fist. "You ladies be nice while I'm gone!" she said. "Especially you, Magda!" But Magda was too busy gobbling up seeds and nudging her fellow hens out of her way to pay any attention to Dervla.

Amelia gently placed Lola in a plastic crate. The poor chicken huddled inside, her head drawn back into her body. Amelia placed the crate on the middle seat of Dervla's jeep, then hopped in beside it. Sam piled in on the other side with the box of eggs, while Mac curled up in the footwell. As the car started off, Lola let out sad little peeps. Amelia

put her hand on the top of the crate, steadying it as best she could.

I really hope Lola will be OK! Amelia thought.

CHAPTER TWO

Inside one of Animal Ark's brightly lit
assessment rooms, Amelia handed Lola's
crate to Mrs Hope, one of the two vets
who owned the practice. Mrs Hope
lifted Lola out on to the examination
table. The hen gave a startled screech
and flapped her wings, but Mrs Hope

gently pinned Lola under her arm.
"Hush, little one," she said, inspecting
the torn comb with a blue-gloved
finger.

At last she looked up with a smile.
"This doesn't look too serious," she said.
"Sam, can you hold her? It won't take
long to tidy her up."

Sam's face turned grave with
concentration as he put his arms around
Lola. Mrs Hope quickly cleaned the
wound with antiseptic. Then she took a
sharp pair of scissors and started to trim
away the damaged part of the comb.
Amelia winced as blood welled from
the cut. Poor Lola let out a squawk of

alarm and tried to flap her wings, but
Sam managed to hold her steady as
Mrs Hope worked. After smearing some
antiseptic cream on the cut, she asked
Sam to pop Lola back into the crate.

"She'll be fine once the wound's
healed," Mrs Hope said. "But she'll need
to be kept on her own until then. How

did the injury happen?"

"The hens had a fight," Sam said.

"Lola's new. One of the old hens attacked her," Amelia added.

"That's right," Dervla confirmed. "I've just adopted some ex-battery hens, but they aren't settling in as well as I'd hoped."

"Ah!" Mrs Hope said, nodding. "In that case, I think the bully hen needs to be separated from the others, too. If she can't push them around, she'll soon get the message that the newcomers are there to stay. In a few days, the new hens will have settled in and everything should be OK."

"Well, that's a relief," Dervla said as they filed back into the waiting room. Mac leapt up from his seat by the reception desk to greet them, his whole body wagging in time with his tail. Kneeling, Sam fended off excited licks with his hands. "I don't suppose Magda's going to be happy, though," Dervla went on, heading for the door. "Would you two like a lift home?"

"Thank you, but it isn't far to walk," Amelia told Dervla. "We'll stay here for a bit to help out. I hope Lola gets better soon."

As Amelia opened the door for Dervla, she heard a chuckle from Julia at the reception desk. "Oh, my goodness!" the receptionist said. "You have to come and see this! It's the cutest thing ever!"

"Down!" Sam said, pushing Mac away from his face, then craning his neck to look at Julia's computer screen. Amelia quickly joined him.

Julia pressed play on the clip she'd been watching. An adorable smoky-grey kitten sprang into action, standing tall on its back paws in front of a mirror, shadow boxing with its own image. It bopped and pawed at the glass, its ears flicked back and its fluffy fur sticking up on end. Then the kitten hunkered down, wiggled its tiny backside and pounced.

It hit the mirror, bounced off and skittered away, wide-eyed and bristling all over.

Mac let out an excited bark. Sam and Amelia giggled.

"That's so adorable!" Amelia said. Then she turned to Sam. "Hey! Maybe *we* should make some funny pet videos for the Animal Ark website."

"That's not a bad idea!" Mr Hope said, carrying an armful of supplies from the store cupboard. "We haven't updated the site for a while. We want to make it fun and friendly to attract new customers to the surgery. A few funny animal videos might be just what's needed." He put down his bundle. "I'll lend you an old phone so you can take some clips."

Sam's eyes shone. "There are so many cool animals in Welford, we're bound to make some epic videos!" he said.

"We'll get loads of people to visit the website!" added Amelia, squeezing her hands together with excitement.

"Here you go," Mr Hope said, holding out a sleek black phone. "Why don't you see if any of our visitors feel like performing – but make sure you get permission first."

"Thank you, we will!" Amelia said.

An elderly man was waiting in the reception area with a cardboard box on his lap. As Sam and Amelia approached him, he looked up, his eyes twinkling.

"Making movies, are you?" he said. "Well, you're welcome to film old Sheldon here, but I warn you, he's not very lively." The man opened the lid of the box.

Inside Amelia could see the top of a

domed green shell. *A tortoise!* she realised. It was fast asleep on a bed of straw.

"I think he might be a bit too quiet," Amelia told the old man. "But thank you anyway."

Just then, a man with a little girl in pigtails tugging at his hand came into the surgery.

"Hello, Anna!" Julia said, smiling at the girl as they approached the reception desk. "Are you here to collect Pogo?" The little girl nodded, grinning. "I'll let Mrs Hope know you're here,"

Julia told the girl's father, picking up the phone.

A moment later Mrs Hope brought out an animal carrier. Through the bars, Amelia could make out a huge lop-eared rabbit with a bandaged paw.

"How's Pogo doing?" the little girl's father asked anxiously.

"Really well," Mrs Hope said. "You can take off the bandages in a day or two."

"Hi, Pogo!" Anna cried, standing on tiptoes and poking a finger through the carrier bars.

"Excuse me," Sam said. "We're making a video for Animal Ark. Please may we film your rabbit – if he's up to it?"

"I don't see why not," the man said, smiling. He got the rabbit out of the carrier and set it down on the tiled floor as Amelia got the phone ready to film. "Anna, why don't you give Pogo a treat," the man said, handing his daughter a scrap of lettuce.

Amelia zoomed in on Pogo.

"And, action!" she said, pressing the record button. The little girl's pudgy hand came into view on the screen, holding the lettuce. Pogo briefly twitched his pink nose at the treat. But then his head sank on to his paws.

"It looks like he's not up to

performing yet," Amelia
said, as the man put
the rabbit back in the
carrier. "But thank you
for letting us try."

After the little girl and her father had
left with Pogo, Amelia frowned and
turned to Sam. "No luck so far," she
sighed. "What now?"

"Now we need to find a natural
performer," Sam said, looking at her
meaningfully. "An animal with real *star*
quality …"

"That's it!" Amelia's hopes lifted as she
thought of her pet kitten. "We can film
Star. She's perfect!"

CHAPTER THREE

Amelia was just going to return Mr
Hope's phone, when the front door to
the surgery swung open. A woman in
a sparkly jumper came in, followed
by a boy holding an animal carrier.
Something scrabbled about inside it,
making a soft squeaking sound. *Maybe*

this will be our new star ... thought Amelia.

The boy had pale blond hair and blue eyes, and Amelia suddenly recognised him. He was a few years below her at school, and she had sometimes seen him standing alone in the playground at break times.

Amelia gave Sam a nudge. "We should go and say hi," she whispered.

"Hello," Sam said as the boy and the woman sat down. "You go to Welford Primary School, don't you?"

The boy peeked through his floppy fringe, and a blush crept over his cheeks.

The woman nodded. "That's right. We live right next door to the school."

"My name's Sam, and this is Amelia," Sam said.

"Aren't you going to say hello, Connor?" the boy's mother prompted.

Connor's eyes had fallen to the carrier on his lap.

Amelia noticed that he looked stiff and uncomfortable. She felt a rush of sympathy. Sometimes she felt shy around older kids, too.

She was just about to ask about the video, when Mrs Hope poked her head around the assessment room door.

"Snap, Crackle and Pop?" she called.

"That will be us!" Connor's mum said, getting to her feet.

Mrs Hope smiled. "Come on through," she said, then turned to Amelia and Sam. "Could you two give us a hand?"

"We're official helpers at Animal Ark," Amelia told Connor, as she and Sam followed him into the assessment room.

Connor put the carrier on the examination table and opened the front to reveal three squat furry bodies snuggled together inside.

"Guinea pigs!" Amelia exclaimed. All three piggies shuffled to the back of the carrier, giving nervous little squeaks. One of them had black and white fur, sticking up in all directions. The smallest of the three was black all over, and the final pig had tufty orange fur.

"Cute!" Sam said.

Connor put his hands into the carrier and scooped out the fluffy orange guinea pig. "Say hello, Pop."

Amelia reached out to stroke Pop's cheek. He snuffled at her sleeve, his whiskers twitching.

"These three need a nail trim, is that right?" said Mrs Hope.

Connor's mum nudged him gently from behind. "Um, yes," he said quietly. "Crackle and Snap have black claws, so we can't see where to cut. And Pop hates having it done. He squirms about too much."

"In that case, let's start with him. Get it over and done with quickly," Mrs Hope said. "Amelia, can you hold Pop firmly around his belly so I can get to his feet?" Amelia put both hands around the guinea pig's middle and lifted him up, showing his furry tummy to Mrs Hope. Pop squeaked and started to wriggle, but Amelia kept a firm grip on him. Mrs Hope took Pop's front paw

between two fingers
and pulled it gently
towards her.

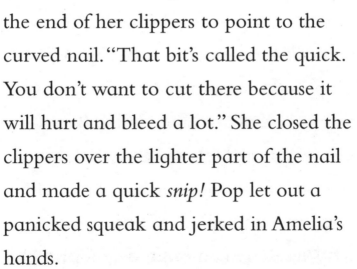

"See here, where
the claw looks
darker near the
base," she said, using
the end of her clippers to point to the
curved nail. "That bit's called the quick.
You don't want to cut there because it
will hurt and bleed a lot." She closed the
clippers over the lighter part of the nail
and made a quick *snip!* Pop let out a
panicked squeak and jerked in Amelia's
hands.

Mrs Hope let out a chuckle. "He

really doesn't like having his nails cut, does he? Well, I promise you I'm not hurting him, and it has to be done."

Soon Mrs Hope had finished trimming all of Pop's nails. Amelia gently handed him to Connor while Sam held Crackle for Mrs Hope. Crackle's nails were black, and Amelia couldn't see the quick at all, but Mrs Hope didn't hesitate. She quickly snipped off all the tips. Unlike Pop, Crackle stayed relaxed the whole time, her black eyes gazing about with interest.

"Why don't you hold Snap for me?" Mrs Hope asked Connor. The young

boy blushed again, but Amelia noticed him smiling proudly as he held the black and white guinea pig still. "If you let them run around on a hard surface every now and then," Mrs Hope said, clipping away, "their claws won't need to be trimmed all that often."

Soon, all three guinea pigs were safely back in their carrier.

Julia poked her head into the room, raising an eyebrow at Sam. "Your mum's on the phone, young man," she said. "Apparently she can't start baking until you get back."

Sam and Amelia looked at each other in alarm. "The eggs!" Sam said.

"Well, off you go then," Mrs Hope said. "Thank you for your help."

"Will you thank Mr Hope for lending us his phone?" Amelia said, quickly handing it to Mrs Hope. "Your guinea pigs are so cool, Connor. See you at school on Monday!"

Sam and Amelia hurried through to the waiting area. Sam grabbed the box of eggs he'd left on Julia's desk, then they set out along the sunny lane.

"Connor is really shy, isn't he?" Sam said as Mac trotted along next to him.

"Well, except when he's talking about his guinea pigs," said Amelia.

"He's lucky to have three pets," said Sam.

"I know," said Amelia. "I keep
thinking about the hens that Dervla
told us about. I wish I could adopt some.
But with Star at home, it would be a
disaster!"

"Same here with Mac," Sam said,
shaking his head. "It's a shame, because
it would be really useful to have the
eggs!"

Amelia frowned. *Who could possibly
adopt those chickens … ?*

CHAPTER FOUR

On Monday after school, Amelia went
to meet Sam at Animal Ark, where they
collected a prescription from Julia. Then
they hurried over to their classmate
Caleb's house. From outside, she could
just see the family's llamas happily
grazing in the field behind the house.

She grinned as she thought of how Caleb had gone from having no pets at all, to having two llamas and two pigs in just a couple of weeks. *The Parishes are animal mad!* she thought with a smile.

Then, all of a sudden, she had a perfect idea. Amelia was just about to tell it to Sam, when Mrs Parish opened the door.

"We've got a delivery for you," Sam said, showing her a box of pig worming medicine.

"Thank you," Mrs Parish said. Then she called up to her son, "Caleb, your friends are here!"

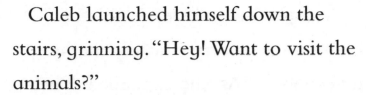

Caleb launched himself down the stairs, grinning. "Hey! Want to visit the animals?"

"We'd love to!" Amelia said. "But first, can we ask you about something?"

Sam gave her a puzzled look.

"Come on in," Mrs Parish said.

Amelia felt her heart thumping as she and Sam followed Caleb and his mum into the farmhouse kitchen. Mrs Parish shoved some magazines aside, so they could sit up at the table. Amelia took out a piece of paper from her back pocket and unfolded it, revealing an information leaflet from the chicken rehoming centre.

"My gran's friend Dervla told us about some factory chickens that need a new home," Amelia explained. "She's taken a dozen in, but there are still lots left. We wondered if you might want to adopt some."

"Oh, Mum! Can we?" Caleb asked. "I could help look after them. And just think – we'd have fresh eggs every day!"

"Great idea, Amelia!" said Sam, grinning. Mrs Parish took the leaflet and put on her reading glasses. "It does sound interesting," she said, when she'd finished reading it through. "But we'd have to think about it. We already have quite a few animals to take care of. Which reminds me – the pigs will be wondering where their dinner is!"

"Can we help feed them?" Sam asked.

"Yes!" Amelia chimed in. "Mr Hope showed us exactly how much worming medicine to measure out for each pig. We could give it to them now."

"Good plan," Mrs Parish said. Caleb led the way through the kitchen into their garden. Beyond a trampoline and a climbing frame, the garden backed

on to a large field. The Parish family's
llamas, Llarry and Lliam, grazed at
the far end. Next door to the llamas,
two huge pigs dozed on their sides in a
muddy pen.

Mrs Parish led the way to the pig pen
and opened a wide gate. Hearing the
screech of metal, Daisy and Pip heaved
themselves up and trotted over, grunting.

Amelia put out her hand and Daisy
nosed at it with her warm, upturned
snout. While Sam and Caleb stroked Pip,
Amelia scratched Daisy behind the ears,
smiling as the pig half-closed her eyes
with pleasure. Then Daisy scrunched up
her face and sneezed.

"Bless you!" Amelia said, giggling.

Mrs Parish led Amelia, Caleb and

Sam through another gate towards the trough. The two pigs squelched through the soft mud after them, pushing up against the gate, snorting eagerly.

"Not long now!" Mrs Parish said, pouring pellets from a big bag into each side of the trough. Amelia carefully measured out a syringe of worming medicine and squirted half on to each pile of feed. Then Mrs Parish opened the gate.

Daisy and Pip bundled in, quickly burying their snouts in the food. Mrs Parish watched them, smiling.

"So, *can* we get some chickens, Mum?" Caleb asked. "We've got loads of space,

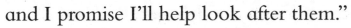

and I promise I'll help look after them."

Mrs Parish gazed out over the wide expanse of grassland behind their house. "We'd need to build a hen house …" she said thoughtfully.

Amelia felt her heart beat quicker. *She's going to say yes!* "Leave that to us!" Amelia said. "Our friend Izzy's mum is a carpenter. I'm sure she'd be willing to help."

"And the chickens have nowhere else to go," Sam added.

Mrs Parish let out a theatrical sigh. "Oh, all right!" she said. "I'll talk to your father, Caleb. I've got a feeling he'll say yes." Then she raised a stern

eyebrow. "But you really will have to take responsibility for looking after them."

Caleb punched the air. "Yes! Of course I will, Mum! It'll be awesome!"

"Actually," Mrs Parish said to Caleb, "since everyone loves stopping by to pet the pigs and llamas, your father and I have been thinking that we could open a petting farm."

"Wow!" said Amelia. "That would be incredible."

"Yeah!" Caleb said, his eyes wide. "We

could get goats and rabbits. Maybe even a donkey."

"Hold your horses!" Mrs Parish said, grinning. "Let's just focus on the chickens for now. I think that'll give us more than enough to do."

Amelia felt excitement bubbling up inside her, and she couldn't stop smiling. *A petting farm would be so cool ... Welford is about to get even more amazing!*

CHAPTER FIVE

As soon as the bell rang for home time on Tuesday, Amelia and Sam hurried into the playground.

"It's so awesome that Caleb's dad agreed they could get the chickens!" Sam said. "I can't wait to start making the hen house!"

"And I can't wait to get home and start filming!" Amelia said. "Star's so funny – we're bound to get a good video."

Amelia spotted a group of younger children on the far side of the playground. They were crowded round a boy with a familiar mop of pale blond hair. "Is that Connor?" she asked, pointing.

"I think so …" Sam said uncertainly. "Wow. I thought he was shy. Now it looks like he's got loads of friends."

Amelia noticed the children were craning over something in Connor's hands – something furry. "I've got a bad feeling about this," she said, as they drew closer. A little girl with curly red hair giggled as she stroked the furry, black and white bundle in Connor's arms.

"Oh no," Sam groaned. "He brought Snap to school."

"The poor thing must be terrified!" Amelia said.

Connor stood grinning proudly as his classmates petted the guinea pig. Snap looked wide-eyed and stiff with fear.

The red-haired girl let out a squeal. "Ew! Gross! He just peed on me!" she said, shoving Snap back towards Connor. The other children laughed and nudged each other. Before long, they drifted apart, heading towards the school gates. Connor nuzzled Snap to his chest, stroking his ears.

As Amelia and Sam approached, the younger boy looked up, smiling. "Hi!"

"Hey," said Amelia. She didn't want to upset Connor, but she knew she needed to say something. "I don't want to get you in trouble, but you really shouldn't bring Snap to school."

Connor's face fell, and red blotches appeared on his cheeks. "But everyone loves him," he said. He opened his bag. "Look, I packed it with straw so he'd be comfortable."

"He must be getting bumped around in there," said Sam. "And it's all dark! He'd be much better off at home."

Connor looked crestfallen. "I guess so." As he shuffled away towards the gates, his shoulders sagged.

Amelia frowned. "I feel bad. I didn't mean to make him unhappy."

"I know," sighed Sam. "He probably

thought it would help him make friends. But it's not fair on Snap! I bet he's been really frightened in there."

Amelia nodded. *Poor Snap!*

"Anyway, we've got some important Animal Ark business," said Sam. He grinned. "Are you ready to start filming?"

Amelia smiled back, pushing her worries aside. She'd been looking forward to this all day long. "You bet!" she said.

Sam collected Mac from the B&B on the way to Amelia's house. As they arrived at the cottage where Amelia lived, her gran met them at the door.

"Hello, Sam! And Mac, of course," she said, bending to pet the little dog.

Amelia hugged her gran. "Can you mind Mac while we make a film of Star?" she asked.

"Ooh! I think I could manage that," Gran said, taking Mac's lead. "I might even be able to find him a treat."

Once Amelia had collected her tablet from her bedroom, she and Sam went in search of Star. They found the tortoiseshell kitten curled up in a strip of sunlight on the living-room rug. As

Amelia approached, Star woke and stretched lazily.

Sam took Amelia's tablet. "Ready?" he asked, crouching down. Amelia took a feathered ball on a stick from the coffee table and dangled it above her kitten.

"Yup!" she said.

"Then … action!" Sam said.

Amelia shook the stick in her hand, making the ball bounce on its string. But Star ignored the toy and stalked up to Sam, rubbing her face on the tablet.

"Get off," Sam said, playfully pushing the kitten away. But Star dodged around his hand and headed straight back to the tablet, rubbing her cheek on the warm screen and purring with pleasure. Then she paced to the window, her tail curled in a question mark, and let out a meow.

"Oh, come on, Star!" Amelia said. "You normally love this toy!" She dangled the ball over the kitten's head again. Star let out another squeaky

meow, pawing at the window pane.

"She wants to go out," Amelia said. "Maybe we'll get a better clip in the garden."

Star led Sam and Amelia through to the kitchen, passing Mac, who was busy chewing on a carrot while Gran chopped vegetables. Amelia opened the back door, then she and Sam followed Star out into the garden. But before Sam could even get the tablet ready to film, Star bounded across the lawn, then up and over the fence.

Amelia let out a groan of frustration. "Great!" she said.

"How about we film Mac instead?" Sam suggested, as the puppy trotted out to meet them. But as Sam lifted the tablet and pressed 'play', Mac whimpered and his ears flattened against his head. Sam tried coaxing his dog, but Mac just crouched at Amelia's feet, lowering his head to the ground and giving a sad little whine.

"This is the school play all over again," Sam said, sighing. "Mac didn't want to star in that, either! Well, I'm not going to film you if you don't like it." He sank on to the grass and patted his lap. Mac bounded over, his short tail whirling around like a propeller.

Amelia laughed as Mac licked Sam's ears and nose, but she couldn't help feeling a bit sad. *Mac doesn't like the tablet at all, and Star likes it way too much! At this rate we'll never get a good video.* Where on earth could they find an animal superstar?

CHAPTER SIX

After school on Thursday, Sam and
Amelia hurried to Animal Ark. The
Hopes had received some free samples
of chicken feed, and they'd agreed that
Sam and Amelia could take it to the
Parishes, to help with the rehoming
project.

Julia greeted them with a broad smile. "I hope you're feeling strong!" she said, patting the two huge bags of chicken feed by the side of her desk. "When are the hens arriving?"

"Around midday on Saturday," Sam said. "Which means we only have Saturday morning to build their coop!"

"I'm sure you two can manage it," Julia said.

"Izzy's mum has already drawn up the design," Amelia said. "And she's got plenty of spare wood. We just need to get a few more volunteers to help." As Amelia spoke, she noticed a strange ball on Julia's desk, sitting amongst a

selection of dog chews and catnip mice.
The little ball was made from woven
twigs.

"What's that?" she asked the
receptionist.

"It's a toy from a manufacturer," Julia
answered. "We get loads of samples sent
in."

Amelia picked the ball up for a closer
look. It fit neatly in her palm. *The perfect
boredom buster for your guinea pig pals*, the
label read. "This would be great for
Connor's guinea pigs," she said.

"They can trial it for us," Julia said.

"Thanks!" Amelia said, slipping the
ball into her pocket. She lifted a bag of

chicken feed. "Whoa!" The weight of it almost tugged her arms from their sockets. She braced herself and hefted it higher, hugging it to her chest. "Let's go, then!" she said, already feeling hot beneath her jacket.

By the time Sam and Amelia had dropped the chicken feed off at Caleb's house, Amelia's arms ached and Sam's face was shiny with sweat. "Just one more delivery to go!" Amelia said, patting the guinea pig ball in her pocket. "But this one isn't so hard to carry."

Sam grinned. "Hopefully, this will make up for telling Connor he needs to leave Snap at home. Come on – I know where he lives."

The two friends headed back along winding country lanes towards their school. They stopped at a bright-looking modern house opposite the school gates. Sam rapped at the knocker.

A moment later Connor answered, his pale face looking more anxious than ever. Amelia held out the ball. "We brought this toy for your guinea pigs," she said. But instead of smiling, Connor swallowed hard, his chin trembling.

"Are you OK?" Sam asked.

Connor shook his head. "It's Snap,"

he said anxiously. "There's something wrong with him!"

Worry knifed through Amelia's gut, but she did her best to sound calm. "Can we see him?" she asked. "Maybe we can help."

Connor led them inside, through a tidy living room which led to a sunny conservatory. A multi-level hutch stood at the back, with straw poking through its wire-mesh windows. Amelia could see Crackle and Pop huddled together, nibbling a carrot. But there was no sign of Snap.

Connor crossed to the hutch and opened a door. Snap sat inside, pressed against the back wall, trembling all over.

"He hasn't been eating or drinking," Connor said. "And he keeps shivering, even when I hold him."

"Have you been taking him into school again?" Amelia asked. Her voice came out more sharply than she'd intended.

"Only one more time," Connor said, his eyes dropping to the floor. "I thought it would be OK."

Amelia looked at the shivering guinea pig. "We'd better take him to Animal Ark," she said. "Guinea pigs can't go for more than a couple of days without food, and if he isn't drinking, either."

She stopped
when she
saw the look
of horror in
Connor's eyes.
"Don't worry,
though – I'm sure it's
not too late. But we should go now. Are
your parents at home?"

Connor shook his head. "Taylor, my
big brother, is looking after me. He's
playing video games upstairs."

"Then ask him if you can go," Amelia
said. "I'm sure the Hopes will sort out
any payment with your parents when
they get back."

"I'll pay with my birthday money if I have to," Connor said. "Anything to make sure Snap's OK!"

Connor disappeared and Amelia heard him call up the stairs to his brother. A low, gruff voice replied, "Sure, whatever."

In a few minutes, Connor had wrapped Snap in a fleece for warmth and put him in his animal carrier. Peeking out from the blanket, his whiskers trembled as he shook all over. The guinea pig looked pitiful.

Amelia's chest tightened with worry. *Please let Snap be OK!*

CHAPTER SEVEN

After an anxious wait at Animal Ark,
they finally heard Mrs Hope call Snap's
name. Connor led the way into the
assessment room and took his guinea
pig out of the carrier.

"Snap hasn't been eating or drinking,"
Amelia told Mrs Hope. "We're worried

that he'll get dehydrated."

Mrs Hope took the trembling guinea pig from Connor. After listening to Snap's chest with a stethoscope and taking his temperature, she felt him all over with her hands. Then she pinched the skin on the back of his neck and watched as it slowly fell back into place.

"His temperature's fine and I'm not worried about an infection," Mrs Hope said. "But he does seem dehydrated, and quite stressed. Has there been any change in his routine?"

Amelia glanced at Connor. The red blotches were back on his cheeks, brighter than ever. "You can tell Mrs Hope," she said gently. "She won't be angry – she just wants to help."

Connor took a deep breath. "I've taken Snap into school a couple of times," he blurted. "I thought if I was there looking after him, he'd be OK."

"Ahh," Mrs Hope said. "I think that explains why Snap's not himself. In the wild, guinea pigs stay together for safety. Being taken somewhere strange and noisy would have made him feel very vulnerable. He needs to be in a familiar place with his friends. Which is good news," she said, stroking Snap's fur. "It means, once I've given him some water, he should be fine. But you'll need to keep him at home from now on."

Mrs Hope picked up a syringe filled with water and cradled Snap in one arm. At first, Snap struggled, turning his head away from the plastic nozzle. But once Mrs Hope had got the first drops

into his mouth, he
seemed to warm to the
idea. His pink tongue
lapped at the syringe
nozzle as he thirstily
drank the water.

"Right!" Mrs Hope
said at last, handing
Snap back to Connor. "He should make
a full recovery, as long as you follow my
advice. But bring him back if you're still
worried."

"Thank you," Connor said, putting
Snap back into his carrier. Amelia and
Sam exchanged relieved smiles, but
Connor still looked miserable, his head

bowed low as he made for the door. *Poor Connor,* Amelia thought. *I wish I could think of a way to cheer him up!*

"Right, let's get Snap back in with his friends," Sam said, as they arrived back at Connor's house.

While Connor opened the hutch, Amelia lifted the guinea pig out of his carrier. As soon as Snap was back inside, Crackle and Pop snuffled around him, making adorable chirping sounds. Snap edged his way towards the water bottle. After a few sniffles and nudges, he started to drink.

Amelia felt a rush of relief. "He's looking better already!" she said.

"Hey, Connor!" called a voice from upstairs.

Amelia and Sam followed Connor upstairs. They stopped outside an open door. A teenager in a hoodie was sitting cross-legged on his bed with a game controller, his face glowing in the light of the TV. He paused his game and nodded at them. "All good with Snap?" He had the same blue eyes and blond hair as Connor, but wore dark-framed glasses.

"He's better now," Connor told his older brother.

As Taylor went back to his game, Connor asked, "Want to see my room?" Amelia and Sam nodded and followed Connor into a small room covered in guinea pig posters. Amelia spotted a photograph on a desk cluttered with model aeroplanes. It showed Connor holding what looked like a much smaller version of Snap. She went over for a closer look.

"Awww!" Amelia cooed. "Snap looks so adorable!"

"That was when I first got him," Connor said. "I was so happy. Today

I was really scared he was going to die. Thank you for helping." He let out a sigh, his face falling.

"So, what's wrong?" Amelia asked. "Are you worried about school?"

Connor nodded, without looking at her.

"But why?" Sam said. "You've got lots of friends. You were talking to a big group of kids at school the other day."

Connor looked glummer than ever. "*Snap's* popular. I'm not."

Amelia wanted to hug the younger boy. But instead, she put her hand on his arm. "You don't need Snap to make friends. You just need to talk to people and find out what you have in common. That's what I did when I started at Welford Primary." Gazing at the model aeroplanes, she suddenly had an idea. "Hey! Do you like building things?"

Caleb nodded.

"Sam and I are helping to make a chicken coop on Saturday at Caleb

Parish's house," said Amelia. "You should come and help!"

"Yeah!" Sam said. "Why don't you invite some kids from your class? The more helpers we have, the better – and it will give you a chance to get to know them."

Connor was just about to reply, when excited squeaks came from downstairs.

"That sounds like Snap!" Connor said, already heading out of the room.

Back in the conservatory, they found the guinea pig pushing his new twig ball around the hutch with his nose while Crackle and Pop watched, their eyes bright with interest.

"Awww!"
Amelia said. "He
really likes that
ball!"

"It looks like
the water did the
trick!" Sam said. "I knew Animal Ark
would be able to help!"

Snap's squeaking got louder and more
insistent as he nudged the ball up a
slope.

"This is so cute!" Amelia said. Then
she had another idea. "Connor, do you
have a camera? We're trying to record a
video for Animal Ark, and I think Snap's
got star quality!"

Connor's face brightened. "Taylor's got a phone. I'll ask him if I can borrow it."

Connor raced off and quickly returned holding a phone in a case decorated with skulls and snakes. He handed it to Amelia.

"Snap knows loads of tricks," Connor said, his eyes shining. "I'll get him to show you." He opened a storage box and took out a low wire fence. Unfolding it, Connor made an enclosure on the ground. Then he quickly set up tunnels, ramps and even a mini see-saw, building an obstacle course inside the enclosure.

Finally, Connor scattered seeds and pellets all around the obstacle course

and set Snap, Crackle and Pop down at
the start. All three guinea pigs scuttled
forwards eagerly, searching for the bits
of food.

Amelia held the phone as steady as
she could, keeping the piggies in shot.
Pop scurried up the first ramp, followed
by Crackle. But, instead of climbing the
ramp, Snap stretched up on his back legs
and snaffled the seeds.

Crackle and Pop disappeared into
the tunnel, each guinea pig emerging
with a well-earned treat. But instead of
going through the tunnel, Snap nudged
it with his nose until all the food rolled
out. He gobbled it up greedily.

Next, he upset the see-saw entirely,
spilling the seeds on to the floor. Amelia
giggled as Crackle and Pop snuffled
around the course, completing each
obstacle in turn, while Snap found
ingenious ways to steal the treats
without finishing a single one.

"Thief!" Sam said, laughing.

Connor grinned proudly as Snap hoovered up the food. "That's my Snap!" he said.

As they stopped filming, Amelia heard a chuckle behind her. She turned to see Taylor watching over their shoulders, grinning. "He's pretty cool, isn't he? If you want, I could put the video online.

I can copy it on to a USB stick for you guys, too."

"Thanks!" said Amelia, handing back the phone. "I think we've found our internet superstar!"

CHAPTER EIGHT

Amelia stood back, shielding her eyes from the sun as she looked at the half-finished chicken house. It was only half past ten on Saturday morning, but they already had the main structure in place, complete with walls, a floor and nest boxes. They just needed to add the

roof and the outdoor run, and the coop
would be ready.

Amelia frowned. *Shame Connor couldn't
make it*, she thought, watching her
friends smiling and laughing as they
worked together.

"Up a bit, Sam," Izzy's mum said, as
Sam held a plank in place for Caleb
to hammer. Inside the enclosure, Izzy
patted straw into the nest boxes.

Just then, Amelia heard distant voices. She glanced towards the Parishes' house and her heart leapt. A smiling Connor was leading a group of children across the garden. As they drew closer, Amelia recognised the red-haired girl and some of the others Connor had been showing Snap to at school.

Amelia raced across the field to meet them. "You came!" she said, taking Connor's arm and tugging him towards the chicken house. "You're just in time to help us put the roof on. That's the trickiest part!"

As soon as they reached the construction site, Izzy's mum gave out jobs. Within minutes, Connor and his friends were busy with screwdrivers and staplers.

Connor held a section of chicken wire against the frame of the outdoor run while Amelia stapled it on.

"Thanks for taking that video of Snap," Connor said. "My brother says it's already had hundreds of views on his online video channel!"

"Wow!" Amelia said. "That's pretty good going for two days!"

"The kids at school loved it," Connor said. "They reckon Snap's going to be famous!"

"Brilliant!" Amelia said, feeling a

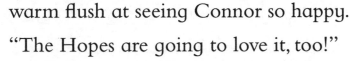

warm flush at seeing Connor so happy.
"The Hopes are going to love it, too!"

Amelia and Connor finished stapling
chicken wire all around the enclosure,
while the others fitted the roof. Once
that was done, Amelia helped Sam
attach tarpaper to the slanted gables.

"I'm glad Connor was brave enough to invite his friends," Sam said in a low voice, pressing the trigger of his stapler.

As Amelia held the rough tarpaper in place, she watched the younger boy chatting to Izzy, his hands tracing shapes in the air as he spoke. Amelia smiled as she saw Izzy put her fists under her chin and wiggle her nose, imitating her rabbits.

"I think it helps that he's found some people who love animals as much as he does," Amelia said. "Hopefully he's realised that he doesn't need to bring Snap into school to make friends – he just needs to be himself!"

Once Sam had stapled the last
corner of tarpaper, Caleb carried the
chickens' sand bath into the coop. As
a final touch, Izzy's mum hammered
a sign Izzy had
painted above
the coop door. It
read *Cluckingham
Palace.*

"Wow! You
guys have been
working hard!"
a deep voice boomed. Amelia turned to
see Caleb's parents striding across their
field. Mrs Parish had a bulging cool bag
slung over her shoulder and Mr Parish

carried two bottles of fizzy drink and a tower of plastic cups.

"Who's hungry?" Caleb's mum said.

Before anyone could answer, Caleb pointed. "Look, the chickens have arrived!"

A van turned into the Parishes' long drive, pulling a livestock trailer filled with plastic crates.

"Lunch had better wait," Mr Parish said. "We're going to need all hands on deck to get the chickens moved into their new home!"

With so many helpers, it didn't take long to unload the new arrivals. Soon, Amelia and Sam sat with their friends

on the grass, demolishing piles of
sandwiches. Amelia watched the chickens
exploring their new home as she ate.
Nervous at first, the hens stayed close
together. Then a few bolder birds edged
away from the rest, pecking at the grass.

Eventually, one plucked up the courage to peek inside the hen house. As soon as she was in, the rest followed, their heads jerking from side to side as they looked around, clucking happily.

"One step closer to a petting farm!" Amelia whispered to Caleb.

"Believe me," said Caleb, "I'm doing everything I can to persuade my parents to go through with the idea."

Amelia grinned. "I can't wait!"

"Ah! There you are," Mr Hope said, as Amelia and Sam filed into the waiting area with Connor. "We've got

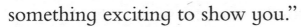

something exciting to show you."

Two weeks had passed since the chickens had moved into their new home. Mr Hope had called Amelia earlier that day, asking her and Sam to come to Animal Ark and to bring Connor.

Sam, Amelia and Connor exchanged puzzled glances as they followed Mr Hope through an open door behind the reception desk and into the practice's office. Mrs Hope stood inside with an open laptop before her. Amelia recognised the Animal Ark website on the screen, but it had been updated with a bolder font and more photographs.

Right near the top of the home page, Amelia spotted Connor's video clip. Mrs Hope set the video rolling, and the three friends watched as Crackle and Pop dutifully completed the course, while Snap cheated his way around each obstacle.

"It's had hundreds of views," Mrs Hope said, grinning. "And three new pet

owners have signed up with the practice already. This video is just what our website needed!"

Amelia smiled as she saw Connor flush with pride.

As they all went back into the waiting area, the front door swung open and Dervla pushed through it, carrying a plastic crate.

"I've brought Lola in for her check-up," Dervla called. "The cut's healed really well."

"That's great news!" Mrs Hope said.

"How's Magda doing?" Amelia asked.

Dervla smiled. "She's back in with the others now. She's still bossy, but all the

hens seem happy and there haven't been any more fights. I suppose they just needed time to settle in."

"It's funny," said Amelia. "Separating your hens solved their problems. But Connor's guinea pigs needed to be together. That's one thing I love about helping here – the animals are all so different!"

"So, are you three sticking around to help with Lola?" Mrs Hope asked.

Amelia exchanged quick glances with

her friends. "Not this time, if you don't mind," she said. "We're going over to Connor's house to help him make a new video of Snap."

"I think we can spare you," Mrs Hope said. "After all, we don't want to keep our guinea pig superstar's fans waiting!"

Snap has loads of fans, but so does Connor! Amelia thought, grinning. She had seen him playing with his friends every break time since they'd helped build the chicken coop. Animals really did help bring people together!

The End

Turn the page for a sneak peek at
Amelia and Sam's next adventure!

ANiMAL ARK

The Lonely Pony

Lucy Daniels

"Here it comes!" gasped Sam Baxter.

Amelia Haywood caught her breath. A chestnut-coloured horse broke into a canter a few metres in front of her. The rider crouched low in the saddle as the horse dashed towards a pyramid of logs lying across the muddy ground. Its muscles flexed under its gleaming coat. Then it sailed over the jump.

"Hooray!" cheered Amelia. She and Sam were sheltering in a marquee next to the muddy race course. It was Amelia's first ever cross-country event, and it was pouring with rain. But even so, excitement buzzed through the crowd.

The next horse and rider trotted on

to the course. Sam glanced at his watch. "There are two-minute gaps between each horse," he explained, raising his voice over the chattering crowd and the rain spattering on the marquee's plastic roof. "It's so they don't get traffic-jams at the jumps."

Amelia grinned. *At least someone knows the rules!* She had seen horse races on TV before, so she'd thought that all the horses would set off together. But in a cross-country race, there was no starting line. Instead, a timer was started when each horse took the first jump and stopped when they reached the end of the course. The horse that did it the fastest won!

The chestnut horse was galloping towards the next jump, made out of a picnic table. Amelia cheered again as the horse leapt over and galloped on into a copse of trees. Then a grey horse streaked up to the first jump, its rider leaning forward, cheeks flushed.

"I wish I knew how to ride!" Amelia said, sighing wistfully.

Sam nodded. "Me too! Hey, shall we see if Mr and Mrs Hope need any help?"

They pulled up the hoods of their raincoats and hurried to the next marquee, their wellies squelching in the mud. The marquee was filled with stalls, and the Hopes were sitting by a trestle table loaded with medical equipment.

"How's it going?" asked Amelia, hurrying over to the two vets.

Mrs Hope smiled and raised a polystyrene cup of tea. "No emergencies, thank goodness!"

"We can all take it easy for now," said Mr Hope.

Amelia felt a rush of pride at the way Mr Hope said "we". She and Sam were official helpers at Animal Ark, the surgery run by the Hopes.

Sam nudged her. "Look at that tiny pony!"

Amelia turned round. A man was leading a golden pony into the marquee.

It was small and sturdy, with a long, shaggy mane. Its tail almost swept the ground!

"Oh!" Amelia squealed in delight. "It's so cute!"

The man led the pony to a stall with a banner that read "Speedwell Pony Homes".

Amelia and Sam glanced at each other, grinned, and hurried over.

"Hello!" said the man, as he took off his wet rain jacket. "I'm Joe. Have you come to meet Ginger?"

Amelia nodded. "Please could we stroke him?"

"Go right ahead," said Joe. "Ginger

loves being petted!"

Ginger was almost the same height as Amelia. A forelock of mane fell over his face, and when Amelia brushed the fringe aside, big, gentle, long-lashed eyes stared back at her. The pony's wide nostrils flared as he nuzzled her jacket. Amelia felt her heart melt.

"What kind of pony is he?" asked Sam, patting Ginger's thick mane.

"He's a Shetland," explained Joe. "He used to be a companion to a racehorse. He and the horse were special friends, and Ginger helped keep him calm before races. But now his owner's moved abroad, so we're trying to find him a new home."

He handed Amelia and Sam a leaflet each. "*Speedwell Pony Rehoming*," Amelia read out loud. "*Matching Ponies with Forever Homes*." Underneath was a photo of Ginger and a phone number.

"Poor Ginger," Sam said.

"Can we help give out the leaflets?" asked Amelia.

Joe beamed. "That's very kind of you! Here, take a pile of them."

As more children gathered to meet Ginger, Amelia and Sam went back to the course, the leaflets in their jacket pockets. The rain had almost stopped, but the ground was slippery under Amelia's wellies.

They walked past the log jump and along the edge of the field, towards a copse of trees. As they passed a jump made of planks of wood fixed between two tree trunks, they heard approaching hoofbeats.

Turning, Amelia saw a big, brown horse with a white stripe on his face thundering down the track, with a young woman on his back. They were getting closer and closer to the jump.

Too close! thought Amelia. Her heart lurched with alarm. *They're going to run straight through it!*

At the last moment the horse threw up his head and jumped. His front legs cleared the plank, but his left back hoof clattered against the fence. *CLUNK!* The horse landed on the other side and stumbled.

"Oh no!" cried Sam.

The rider slid from his back as the horse jerked his head and tottered on three legs. She hung on to the horse's reins, her face creased with worry under her black riding helmet. "Whoa, Walnut!" she said.

"The horse is limping," said Sam. "He needs help!"

"We're going to get the vets!" Amelia called over to the rider.

"Please hurry!" she called back.

Amelia's heart pounded as they sprinted to the marquee – and not just from the effort. She was worried about the horse and the tent seemed a very long way away. *We've got to get there fast*, thought Amelia as she ran, *before that horse hurts itself any more!*

Read **The Lonely Pony** to find out what happens next...

Animal Advice

Do you love animals as much as Amelia and Sam? Here are some tips on how to look after them from veterinary surgeon Sarah McGurk.

Caring for your pet

1. Animals need clean water at all times.
2. They need to be fed too – ask your vet what kind of food is best, and how much the animal needs.
3. Some animals, such as dogs, need exercise every day.
4. Animals also need lots of love. You should always be very gentle with your pets and be careful not to do anything that might hurt them.

When to go to the vet

Sometimes animals get ill. Like you, they will mostly get better on their own. But if your pet has hurt itself or seems very unwell, then a trip to the vet might be needed. Some pets also need to be vaccinated, to prevent them from getting dangerous diseases. Your vet can tell you what your pet needs.

Helping wildlife

1   Always ask an adult before you go near any animals you don't know.

2   If you find an animal or bird which is injured or can't move, it is best not to touch it.

3   If you are worried, you can phone an animal charity such as the RSPCA (SSPCA in Scotland) for help.